I set off one morning in my little red canoe.
My dog wagged his tail.
"Can I come, too?"

"You bet," I said.
"A trip for two—just me and you."

I dipped my paddle into ribbons of blue.
Beaver stopped chewing.
"Can I come, too?"

"There's not much room. It's a one-dog canoe."
But with a slap and a swim,
Beaver scrambled in.

I swished past ferns where dragonflies flew.
Loon stretched her wings.
"Can I come, too?"

"I doubt you'll fit. It's a one-beaver, one-dog canoe."

But with a "woo-hooo!"—flap—
Loon landed on my lap.

Silently we glided under silver webs of dew.
Wolf peered from the pines.
"Can I come, too?"

"Maybe next time! It's a one-loon,
one-beaver, one-dog canoe."

But like an arrow on the wind,
Wolf bounded in.

Still I paddled on in my little red canoe.
Bear slid down a tree.
"Can I come, too?"
"We're pretty darn full! It's a one-wolf,
one-loon, one-beaver, one-dog canoe."

But with a grunt, thump, ka-wump!—
Bear dropped on his rump.

I J-stroked and C-stroked.
What else could I do?
Moose lifted his head.
"Can I come, too?"

"You'll do us all in! It's a one-bear,
one-wolf, one-loon, one-beaver,
one-dog canoe!"

But with a toss of his rack,
Moose climbed in the back.

We teetered and tottered. I glared at my crew.

Frog hopped to a rock.
"Can I come, too?"

"Frog, can't you see? It's a one-moose, one-bear, one-wolf, one-loon, one-beaver, one-dog canoe!"

But with a leap . . .

Plop!

Swoosh-a-bang flop!

We sputtered, splashed, swam . . .
drip-dried on the sand.
"Sorry," Beaver said.
"We should have listened to you.
Guess you were right, it *is* a one-dog canoe."
I started to grin. "It's okay—we had a good swim!"

Then together we bailed till my vessel was dry—
and with a push-a-swoosh—glide—
we waved goodbye.

I set off that evening
as the Northern Lights grew . . .

just me and my pal
in a one-dog canoe.